# DOGS
## IN
## DISGUISE

In memory of my mum, who loved dogs
(especially small, daft dachshunds)

**P.B.**


For Jessica and Hannah

**J.B.**

First published in hardback by HarperCollins *Children's Books* in 2021

HarperCollins *Children's* Books is a division of HarperCollins*Publishers* Ltd
1 London Bridge Street, London SE1 9GF

www.harpercollins.co.uk

HarperCollins*Publishers*
1st Floor, Watermarque Building, Ringsend Road, Dublin 4, Ireland

1 3 5 7 9 10 8 6 4 2

Text copyright © Peter Bently 2021
Illustrations copyright © John Bond 2021

ISBN: 978-0-00-846914-6

Printed and bound in Italy by Rotolito S.p.A.

# DOGS
## IN
## DISGUISE

# BY PETER BENTLY
# & JOHN BOND

HarperCollins *Children's Books*

DOGS come in all kinds of
COLOURS and SIZES,

BUT when no one's looking they put on DISGUISES.

They **DRESS UP** in clothes that they find in their **HOUSES**,

like
**JACKETS**
and
**WAISTCOATS**
and
**SILK SPOTTY BLOUSES.**

**HATS**
and
**HIGH HEELS**
help to make
them look
big –

and sometimes they'll stick
on a **BEARD** or a **WIG.**

**POOCHES** love mooching about at the store,

where **NO DOGS ALLOWED** is the sign on the door.

But who's in that **SWEATER?**
It's Sadie the **SETTER.**

PAY HERE

And there, in
**PINK TROUSERS?**

A pair of **OLD SCHNAUZERS.**

It's **STRICTLY NO DOGS**
at the Café Celeste,

and you aren't
allowed in if
you're
not smartly
dressed –

like this
elegant gent
in the
**TRENCHCOAT**
and **HAT.**

It's a family of **FRENCHIES!**
Well, just fancy that!

PEREGRINE PUG,
in **TUXEDO** and **'TASH**,
is already there
scoffing sausage
and mash.

For **DOGS** who like sport, there's a very tough rule: **ALL DOGS** are **BANNED** in the gym and the pool.

3m

**BUT** no one spots **SPIKE** having fun with the woggles, **DISGUISED** in his bright orange **SWIMSUIT** and **GOGGLES**.

And the folk in the gym cheer the champ at **JUJITSU** –

if only they knew it was **CHARLENE** the **SHIH–TZU!**

The **DOGS** all start early to learn **DRESSING-UP.**

The grown-up **DOGS** teach
it to every young **PUP**.

Sometimes the youngsters aren't terribly wise
and forget that they're meant to be
dressed in **DISGUISE**.

GNU

"GNUS?" laughed the keeper. "You're pulling my leg.

Gnus don't chase squirrels – or SIT UP and BEG!"

And when folks had a barbecue down at the park,
BARNEY THE BEAGLE went too, for a lark.

He thought he'd
sneak in as a
very small tree
and snaffle a
nice tasty
BURGER or THREE.

Poor **BARNEY.**

He ended up feeling a fool

because he'd forgotten a

**VERY BIG** rule:

of all **DOG DISGUISES,**

a tree is the **WORST** . . .

Unless you tell **ALL** of the other dogs **FIRST!**

But most **DOG DISGUISES** are cunning and smart.

They're stunningly skilful at looking the part.

So the next time you're somewhere
that **DOGS** are **FORBIDDEN**,
there are sure to be **POOCHES**,
all cleverly hidden.

Those soldiers lined up on parade in the sun?
Look a bit closer. They're **DOGS**, every one!

And who's **MUNCHING** snacks at the matinee show?

It's those **FRENCHIES** again, sitting all in a row!

And it's not just on Earth that
the **DOGS** wear **DISGUISE** –

just take a look

way up there in the skies.

Who's in the rocket ship off to the **STARS?**